Ginger
and
Chrysanthemum

Kristen Mai Giang  *illustrated by* Shirley Chan

LQ
LEVINE QUERIDO
MONTCLAIR · AMSTERDAM · NEW YORK

Ginger and Chrysanthemum are cousins.
They're as close as two beans in a pod.
But that doesn't mean they always get along.

Ginger and Chrysanthemum are so excited. It's Grandma's birthday. And her two little soybeans want it to be perfect.

"I made a checklist for the party, Ginger. First, we have to…"

"DRESS UP!"

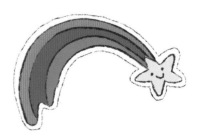

Ginger has no idea what to wear. She tries every color, shimmer, and stripe in her closet.

Chrysanthemum knows exactly what to wear. She puts on her favorite dress she packed the night before, then picks two matching headbands.

Two beans in a pod!

Chrysanthemum checks her list. "We still have to shop *and* decorate."

Tonight, the whole family will celebrate at Grandma's restaurant, where the girls love to help out, surrounded by noodles and soups and dim sum and sweet buns.

To Do List

- ☑ pack outfit
- ☐ meet with Ginger
- ☐ buy decorations
- ☐ pick gift
- ☐ go to grandma's
- ☐ decorate!!!
- ☐ give present
- ☐ have fun!

"There's so muto DO," Ginger cries. "Let's GO!"

Ginger and Chrysanthemum love the crowded aisles
and booths of the market.

"LANTERNS!" Ginger quickly picks paper lanterns in every color.
"Grandma loves flowers." Chrysanthemum reads all the signs.

Meanwhile, Ginger balances the lanterns on her head like hats.

Chrysanthemum decides at last. "Ginger and chrysanthemum flowers – like us."

Together, they choose a jade pendant for Grandma's present.

Two beans in a pod!

At Grandma's New Asian Kitchen, Ginger loves the steamy dumpling counter, where she pounds dough with a *BANG BANG BANG.*

Chrysanthemum prefers the burbling tea station,
where she neatly packs leaves for calming tea.

But today, they're decorating!

Ginger swirls and clatters, hanging lanterns helter-skelter.

Chrysanthemum places one ginger and one chrysanthemum blossom at each table.

Everything is going perfectly, when Grandma gives them a special assignment.

"Who wants to make birthday cake?"

"Me! I'll make an AMAZING cake with BLAZING candles!"
Ginger shouts.

"I'll make a cake light and cool as a cloud," Chrysanthemum
declares.

"Why don't you work *together*, my little soybeans?" asks
Grandma. "Here's my recipe for green tea cake."

Two beans in a pod! How hard can it be?

Chrysanthemum makes a checklist of what to do. Step 1, Step 2…
BANG BANG BANG! Ginger grabs bowls, spoons and pans.
Chrysanthemum covers her ears. "Ginger, you're too loud!"
"Another list?" Ginger can't believe it.

Chrysanthemum takes a deep breath and arranges her measuring cups, littlest to biggest.

BANG BANG BANG! Ginger splashes flour, sugar and eggs everywhere.

Chrysanthemum covers her cups. "Ginger, you're too messy!"

"I'm practically done!" Ginger huffs.

Chrysanthemum steams like a teapot. She reaches for the green tea powder.

   BANG BANG BANG! Ginger grabs the green tea powder and dumps it in.

"Ginger!" Chrysanthemum shrieks. "You're not following the recipe!"

"A recipe is just a fancy list," Ginger grumbles.

Suddenly, Ginger's spoon splats. "OOPS!"

Cool as a winter melon, Chrysanthemum snatches the spoon and flicks it. "You're too fast! Now we have to start over!"

Hot as a chili pepper, Ginger roars, "YOU'RE TOO SLOW!"

Ginger and Chrysanthemum look at the mess. Two beans in a pickle!

"I need a BREAK!" Ginger gets her favorite ice cream – ginger.

"I need tea!" Chrysanthemum gets her favorite tea – chrysanthemum.

"The party's ruined." Chrysanthemum slumps. "There's no cake!"

"We'll make another one," Ginger shrugs.

"But you used all the green tea!" Chrysanthemum sighs.

"Sometimes slowing down in the beginning is faster in the end."

"Huh? You sound like a fortune cookie," Ginger says. "And Chinese people don't even write those."

But she does feel bad. Ginger thinks quickly. "Can we use CHRYSANTHEMUM tea?"

Chrysanthemum's eyes light up. "And ginger ice cream for the icing."

"A ginger and chrysanthemum cake!"

The girls giggle, sharing tea and ice cream. Two beans in a pod!

With happy bellies, the cousins get cooking.
Ginger cleans the mess, *BING BANG BOOM!*

Chrysanthemum carefully measures the ingredients.
Ginger mixes. Chrysanthemum pours.

They both lick the spoon. "Yum!"

The cake looks a little lopsided, the color slightly strange.
Grandma takes the first bite.
Ginger and Chrysanthemum hold hands – and their breath.
She loves it!

"You made a new recipe together. I've never tasted anything like it!"
The whole family laughs and cheers.
Ginger and Chrysanthemum give Grandma her present.
She gives them a big hug. "Thank you, my little soybeans."

The party is a hit.
Ginger and Chrysanthemum share a slice
of their strange, lopsided cake.
Warm cake, cool icing.
Perfect together.

Like two beans in a pod.

party was a success!

Author's Note

In traditional Chinese belief, foods have either warming or cooling characteristics (for example, good to eat when you have a cold or fever), ideally creating balance. As you may have guessed, ginger is a warm food, and chrysanthemum is a cool food. This was my inspiration for the characters Ginger and Chrysanthemum.

To my own little pod, John, Kylie, & Ethan. —KMG

For my grandma, who fed and raised me. —SC

This is an Arthur A. Levine book
Published by Levine Querido

LQ
LEVINE QUERIDO

www.levinequerido.com • info@levinequerido.com

Levine Querido is distributed by Chronicle Books LLC

Text copyright © 2020 by Kristen Mai Giang
Illustrations copyright © 2020 by Shirley Chan

Library of Congress Control Number: 2019909524

ISBN 978-1-64614-001-5

Printed and bound in China

Published in October 2020
First Printing

Book design by Semadar Megged
The text type was set in ITC Galliard Std

Shirley Chan created the artwork digitally using Photoshop and a Wacom tablet.